S0-BMZ-368

Date Due

57670
Bruckberger

St. Procopius College Library
Lisle, Ill.

THE SEVEN MIRACLES OF GUBBIO

AND THE EIGHTH

THE
Seven Miracles of Gubbio

AND THE EIGHTH

A Parable

BY RAYMOND LEOPOLD BRUCKBERGER, DOMINICAN

Translated from the French by Gerold Lauck

Illustrated by Peter Lauck

WHITTLESEY HOUSE

McGraw-Hill Book Company, Inc · New York & Toronto

Theodore Lownik Library
Illinois Benedictine College
Lisle, Illinois 60532

843.
B888s

THE SEVEN MIRACLES OF GUBBIO AND THE EIGHTH

Copyright, 1948, by R. L. Bruckberger. All rights reserved. This book, or parts thereof, may not be reproduced in any form without permission of the publisher.

Published by Whittlesey House

A division of the McGraw-Hill Book Company, Inc.

Printed in the United States of America

57670

Preface by the Translator

THIS simple yet subtle little miracle story appeared in a French magazine, Le Cheval de Troie, Paris, in September, 1947, entitled Le Loup de Gubbio.

I read it snowbound during last Christmas week at my home in Princeton and its beauty made such a deep penetration that I could not dismiss it from my mind. Three thousand miles separated me from the monastery at St. Maximin, France, where the author wrought this little work of art, but we were together in mind and emotion that blustery winter day at my fireside.

So, despite my limitations and my adherence to a communion other than that of Le Père Bruckberger, the Dominican who wrote it, I could not resist the desire to translate.

I did have for it a devoted love of story and its telling, and this served as self-excuse for essaying the hazards of conveying in English this so delicate and misleadingly simple little allegory founded on one of St. Francis's miracles recounted in old Italian in the famous Fioretti or "Little Flowers" of *St. Francis of Assisi. I hope that its beauty will filter through the veil of my translation and serve to warm and gently move the reader.*

To those who have the opportunity, I earnestly recommend the story in its original telling.

The troubled world is indebted to Le Père Bruckberger, this good man of letters, for a story that well may become a French classic. I am very grateful that Le Père Bruckberger has permitted me to be his first translator.

GEROLD LAUCK

La Chaumière, Princeton, N. J.

[6]

THE SEVEN MIRACLES OF GUBBIO

AND THE EIGHTH

And though I have the gift of prophecy, and understand all mysteries, and all knowledge; and though I have all faith, so that I could remove mountains, and have not charity, I am nothing. I COR. XIII, 2.

Oh he that never sought transitory gladness, he that never occupied him in the world, how good a conscience would he keep. IMITATION OF CHRIST, BOOK I, CH. I.

HERE NOW is the story of the Wolf of Gubbio and of his seven miracles. Gubbio is a village in Italy, and one that St. Francis of Assisi loved. It so happened that one winter, a very long time ago, Gubbio was struck by a frightful catastrophe. In a neighboring forest was a young wolf. Never had been seen wolf more daring or so strong. He would swoop down on the sheep and, with the speed of lightning, tear the throat of the most plump ewe and carry her off from the very center of the flock. Obviously there were shepherds and many dogs to guard the sheep. But the wolf was so ferocious that this was no safeguard. Protected or not, all to him was good prey. It seems exaggeration to call a catastrophe just the maraudings of a bad wolf. But when each night one or two ewes were missing on the return of the flock to the sheepfold, and every two weeks a shepherd failed to come home, it assumed very quickly the dimensions of a catastrophe for so small a village. At last no one, man or beast, dared venture beyond the walls of the little town. It was then that they made appeal to St. Francis.

The Poor One came, armed only with his candor and his gentleness. The entire population of Gubbio surged to him as toward a refuge. The Podesta, as the chief magistrate is called, read a long discourse describing the plight of the village. The Saint visited the church to commune with God, and then he quietly wended his way toward the forest. The crowd accompanied him to the gates of the town. There they left him respectfully to proceed alone on the road.

Arriving at the edge of the woods, St. Francis called three times, in his very soft voice, "Brother Wolf!" From very far, on the ramparts of the town, the people of Gubbio watched with anxious curiosity. There was suddenly an immense chill and thrill when they saw the wolf, with great leaps, bolt from the wood. What an animal, magnificent and cruel! His flaming eyes and his hair bristling with rage were enough to make one believe that he was the devil in person. St. Francis advanced like a child. The fright of the crowd turned to awe when they saw the wolf calmed, close his horrible mouth and approach meekly, head lowered, like a dog who wishes to be fondled. The Saint stroked him slowly and quietly and then said in somewhat these words:

"Brother Wolf, much evil has been spoken of you in this country. The Podesta has made a speech as long as it is lamentable against you. It appears that a day does not pass but that you slaughter a creature of God. And not only do you throttle animals, but it is said that you do not even spare men who are made in the image of God, nor the little children without sin, and who have the holy water of baptism still shining pure on their countenances. Brother Wolf, I suffer much grief for your crimes. I know well that if you could speak you would say to me that a famished stomach has no ears for pity, but on the contrary very avid eyes for the feast, and that after all you are a beast of prey, and that your role is to dominate by terror this forest and the fields about it. Nevertheless, I love you, Brother Wolf, and I prefer that you do not talk; you would utter only stupid excuses. But I see by your mouth and the movement of your ears that you understand me very well, and I see also from

the tongue that licks my hands that you like me a little.

"You are right, Brother Wolf, and we two might make a real pair of friends if we became, one and the other, servants of our sweet Lord Jesus Christ, who has given His peace to the world. This peace I come to propose to you, Brother Wolf. But as you do not wish to live on grass or the air of the wind, let us make an agreement between us. On my side I undertake to see that you are fed and nourished by the town of Gubbio, of which you will become a citizen, in all wolfly honor, under the protection of its laws and its magistrates. None shall have the right to enslave or to brutalize you. You will be the Citizen Wolf of Gubbio. But on your side, you must pledge yourself not only never to kill or wound a living soul, but to respect and defend loyally with all your proud courage, the inhabitants of this town, its guests and allies, and the property of each and all of the village. And if, Brother Wolf, this pact is to you agreeable, put your right paw in my right hand, as a sign that you accept all the clauses of our treaty, and that we will undertake faithfully to discharge all our mutual obligations, unto death."

Thereupon St. Francis caused the Podesta to advance, a little pale from the solemnity of the moment, to record and witness the understanding between them, and the wolf put his long silky paw in the hand of St. Francis, who spoke to him again:

"Citizen Wolf of Gubbio, my very sweet brother, each day of your life recall that you have had your paw in my hand, and that I have received your wolfly promise. To reward you for your loyalty, I give you power, in the name of God, witness of our alliance, to perform seven miracles with this right paw of yours that has sealed our oath. Come with us, Brother Wolf, and may the Lord God protect us from all evil, and bless us in his joy."

AND with the acclamation of the people the Wolf of Gubbio was introduced into the city.

It was for Gubbio a day of rejoicing. The streets were decked with bunting, the bells of all the churches and chapels ringing and reverberating in full glory. The children shouted, stamping with joy, and ran before the procession, waving little flags. Along the route, young girls, with eyes shining like diamonds, coifed with costly pointed headdresses, shoulders draped in lace, leaned from the balconies throwing armfuls of flowers on the gay parade. The band played a triumphal march.

It was the Wolf's first contact with civilization, and to tell the truth, he was at the same time both dazed and intoxicated by it all. Everyone brought him something to eat. Secretly, each had a little fear that he might be hungry. In short, he ate enough for four, and at nightfall he lay down in a corner in the house of the Podesta. For the first time in his life his stomach was heavy with plenty. He had almost lost the recollection of his great trees and his den. He slept a sleep without dreams.

Someone suggested it would be just as well, nevertheless, to watch him and to assign an armed guard for protection. The Podesta replied somewhat pompously in character of the village chief who well understood his responsibilities: "It is unnecessary. We will take care of him. The essential is that he must never be hungry."

Whereupon the Podesta himself went to bed. He saw to it, though, that the doors of his room were very carefully locked.

The disposition of wolves is rather curious. They sleep only when they are surfeited, and only hunger awakens them. That is why for the most part wolves never sleep. That was why this particular morning the wolf wakened very late. He was very surprised to find himself under a ceiling. It took him a moment to realize his situation. But as they had put a good and copious plate of food alongside him, he commenced to eat to give respite to his reflections. Then he remembered St. Francis and the promises they had exchanged. As he was of a nature little given to hesitation, he found it unnecessary to return to that which had been, but only to examine his new existence. He went out to take a stroll.

He decided to take a good look at Gubbio. The evening before he had seen very little. He had been too dumbfounded. It was a little town, its walls all white, its roofs reddened by the sun, with wistaria climbing all the railings and balconies of the houses. The light on the rounded cobblestones and against the light-colored houses was so joyous that none might go out into the streets without a smile. Thus the Wolf, seeing all the people of the village so gentle and so gay, could not imagine that it was truly such beings whom he had crunched so cruelly.

"I was mad," said he to himself. "One never reflects enough on what one does. Happily, St. Francis was here."

And he also started to smile, but not enough to show the length of his fangs. "It is necessary to give them time to become accustomed to me," he told himself.

A new sentiment invaded him slowly. It was tenderness. He sensed that he had suddenly become quite a different wolf.

He found himself by chance trotting gaily on a little shaded village square, which bordered on a very deep ravine. Some children were playing ball. He began to play with them and the group was soon in a frenzy of enjoyment. Suddenly a clumsy throw bounced the ball beyond the top of the stone parapet above the steep decline. A little boy leaned over the parapet to regain the ball and lost his balance. The Wolf, very promptly, bounded to the child and caught him by the bottom of his trousers. But the cloth gave way, and to the great shock of all his comrades, the child was precipitated into the abyss.

The Wolf also stood looking, terror-stricken, and suddenly, unconsciously he lifted his right paw. Then was seen a most extraordinary sight. The child's giddy fall was interrupted and he remained motionless between heaven and earth, with his little round behind shining in the sun. Some men, attracted by the cries, arrived, threw a rope, and the child was hoisted to the surface, safe and sound. This then was the first miracle of the Citizen Wolf of Gubbio. It is narrated in all the annals of the town. It is even said that from that day on, the inhabitants of the city had such a veritable veneration for their wolf, that thereafter he was always called "The Holy Wolf."

It isn't to be disputed that selfishness and gratitude are often intertwined. For the Wolf still had at his disposal six more miracles. Those we now describe were infinitely profitable to the common weal. One day he saved a great flock of sheep. Here is how:

He often accompanied the shepherds to the pastures. They knew thus the sheep were well protected. He got on excellently with the dogs, and trained them to hunt wolves; taught them so well, in fact, that no wolf dared poke even the end of his cunning snout outside the forest. It was from this training that the dogs of Gubbio gained such a great reputation for wolf hunting. But that is not what we set out to tell you.

One day when a large flock of sheep grazed tranquilly on the bank of a torrent, the stream swelled suddenly and in a few minutes—as happens in these regions—the flood invaded the ravine. The whole flock, dogs and the shepherds, were about to be drowned, but (as Moses with his rod at the Red Sea) the Wolf, with a gesture of authority, struck the torrent with his paw and the water stayed, and stood like a rampart away from the flock. The herd passed peacefully, and through the liquid wall the fish gazed with wide rounded eyes at the miraculous procession.

ONE MORNING Gubbio was shaken by an earthquake. All the houses threatened to collapse. The Wolf was up and about for he was habitually an early riser. He ran with great speed through all the streets of Gubbio, and it sufficed that he put his right paw on the façade of a building to stabilize it immediately.

The Wolf of Gubbio was now certainly the most honored citizen of the city. The Podesta gave him the right to enter the church, for there was no denying the House of God to a wolf who performed miracles, was a friend of St. Francis, and was favored with most extraordinary grace. Especially as Jesus Christ himself had at His birth in the manger the assistance of two less noble animals.

The Wolf went from house to house. Everywhere he was made at home and treated with respect and gentleness. He was truly happy, and popularity had not corrupted the simplicity of his heart. For within himself he attributed all the merit of his miracles and of his happiness to St. Francis, the soft blessing of whose saintly hand lingered vividly in his recollection and whom he invoked often in his wolf-thought. At night he bedded near a fireplace, closed his eyes,

[23]

put his head on his forepaws, and grunted softly. The people of the house lowered their voices and said, "The Holy Wolf dreams." In reality he prayed. This is what he said in his heart:

"St. Francis of Assisi, great Saint, my very good master and sweet friend, it is I, your brother wolf who speaks to you. I am but a beast, but I know that you hear and understand me far away or near. I thank you joyously for what you have given me. Without you I should never have imagined that men would be so gentle, nor that a wolf could come to an understanding with them and be so happy. I am so well treated, so well fed, and received everywhere with so much honor. I owe it all to you. My desire is not to commit fault in so much happiness. It is true, I believe, that I love the world. It is so agreeable. But I love you above all, and I would cut off my right paw if I should break the promise that I have given you, on my honor as a wolf. Wherever you are, think sometimes of me, and do not permit me ever to merit your anger. If you find one day that this life is bad for me, cause me to be again a poor wolf of the woods. I should prefer to die of hunger all alone rather than offend you or give you pain."

Thus prayed the Wolf of Gubbio in the sincerity of his savage soul. And as often happens when one prays fervently, he little realized what he was asking, or what might be the consequences of his prayer. That is why he had much unhappiness, which now must be recounted.

IT WAS his good heart that brought about the trouble. At this time he lodged in a large house where there were a number of children and many servants. It was an opulent house and very gay. Nevertheless, among the children there was a little girl named Formicella, who had the most crushing misfortune that can come to a little girl in this world. She was ugly, frightfully ugly, as ugly as sin. Her awkward body was deformed. Her legs were twisted and she was a hunchback. Her face was marked with black spots and warts. Her eyes squinted and her hair was coarse as straw. She had webbed hands, like a frog, and ears long and hairy like a daughter of King Midas. Only her voice was beautiful, remarkably beautiful, pure as an oboe and as resonant as the reeds of an organ. No one liked to look upon her, and everyone spoke to Formicella harshly. Even her mother did not love her. (What a visitation, what constant reproach, to have a daughter so ugly!) The little girl was, therefore, always alone, clothed like a slattern. She never ate with the family, but on a little table in a corner of the kitchen. She was never permitted in winter to approach the fireside, nor in the summer allowed outside to play. She had a little dirty attic for her bedroom, and it was in this wretched hovel

that she passed her days, sleeping, or, with fore-
head pressed against the windowpane, watching
the passers-by in the street, crying or sometimes
singing sadly to herself.

This is the way the Holy Wolf came to know
of her existence. The house was nearly empty
and silent at the end of a broiling summer after-
noon. He, himself, was dozing lightly. He heard
a voice that seemed as if it came from Heaven,
so exquisite that he believed he dreamed. He
shook himself. The voice was so beautiful and
the song so sad that he simply had to investigate.
He went up into the garret. Formicella's door
was half open. He pushed it slowly. She saw him,
hid her face in her hands, and melted into tears.
He was deeply touched and remained close to
her. He licked her hands as he had St. Francis's.
She caressed him and thus first experienced the
joy of loving a fellow being without being re-
pulsed. Her face had such a tender smile, if one
had only seen it! They became good friends.

One morning the Wolf entered her room.
Formicella was still asleep. He sat beside her
pillow and watched her with his tender Holy
Wolf eyes. Her little rumpled face was half
veiled by wisps of her tousled hair. Suddenly he
raised his right paw and, still intently watching
Formicella, he waited.

It commenced with her hair. Marveling, he

saw the curls soften, lengthen, assume a golden
color, and begin to shine. Through the light
golden cloud of her tresses, he saw her face
transfigured. All deformity had disappeared. He
saw the lovely curve of her eyebrows, the delicate
shape of her nose, the proud line of her lips.
Her ears took on the pink of a snail's shell.
Formicella awakened and she smiled. Such a
smile! Never would he forget this smile from
the heart of the little girl still unconscious of her
loveliness, expressed at last in such splendid
shining beauty. And her eyes had become so
beautiful, so pure, shaded by long lashes, heavy
and mysterious. She saw her hair and did not
believe that it was hers. She looked at her hands;
they were long, fine hands, soft as satin, white,
made for the harp or delicate lace making.

Formicella bounded from her bed. She did
not have a mirror in her room. Before this miracle
what purpose would it have served? Now she
dressed quickly and made haste to find a mirror.
The miracle continued. And each garment that
she put upon her became itself of a precious
material, beautifully fashioned. How lovely she
was, dressed like a little queen, so straight and
slender of body. She rushed down the stairs,
burst into her mother's room, and stood before
the mirror. She remained a moment with wide-

open gaping mouth in a sort of stupor, striking
her breast with her little hand to see if she was
not still asleep, if all was not false—a dream.
Finally she cried out in a joyous voice:

"Mother, I am so happy! I believe I am going
to die!"

She was very pale, her lips trembled, and two
large tears rolled down her cheeks. She was still
more beautiful in the disarray of her joy. She
collapsed in a faint.

Her mother at first had not recognized her.
Then, hearing the beautiful voice which had
remained unchanged, she realized that this re-
splendent creature, so well formed and so well
dressed, was actually her daughter. But mothers,
even the least tender, always have an infallible
instinct to recognize their own. It was truly
Formicella. She bent with anguish over this
marvelous little doll, placed her gently on the
bed, and assembled the household. They came.
Everyone came. They rejoiced, they cried out,
they swirled around her, someone brought smell-
ing salts, and finally Formicella opened her eyes
and said:

"The Wolf, the Holy Wolf. Mother, it is he
who has healed me of my ugliness!"

They sought the Wolf. He had gone to guard
the sheep and did not return until late in the

evening with the flock. When he came, Formicella took his head in her lovely hands and kissed
him between the eyes, laughing and crying at the
same time, like one crazed.

FROM THEN ON Formicella and the Wolf were never apart. Who saw one saw the other. Often they went walking in the mountains. She, with her parasol, formed a bright red spot in the meadow, and he a black and shining spot on the highway. Obviously he didn't talk. But she sensed his good wolfliness, and then she loved him for all the beauty he had given her. Formicella reigned now, not only in her household, over her brothers, her sisters, her relatives, but her presence was sought at every party in the town. The Wolf accompanied her on these occasions. She always gave him a place of honor. He greatly enjoyed these parties, the boys playing games, the beautiful dancers, and the elegant young girls laughing and romping! In short he had become very worldly. But since he had decided to become a civilized wolf, why not be gentle and gay when everyone liked and respected him? There was no harm in that. St. Francis had asked him never to kill anyone. He had kept his promise. And now it was even very easy for him for he had a tranquil conscience and slept each night the sleep of the just.

Nowhere was there a more waggish fellow than our Wolf. One was never bored with him. They had taught him a hundred conventions of society. In fact he invented some. Above all he wished to give pleasure to Formicella. She was the permanent witness of his miraculous power. He was more proud of her than if he had arrested the sun in its course. Not only was he very strong, but also adroit. So he learned to serve champagne. He held the bottle between his paws, pulled off the wire with his fangs, inclined the bottle knowingly, and lifted the cork without a sound and without spilling a single drop. He held the neck of the bottle with his teeth and poured. He even drank a little himself on occasion. The sparkling taste pleased him and raised his spirits.

One beautiful night they were on the veranda at the home of the Podesta. The magistrate wore a round hat covered with red plush and decked out with medals. Seated apart on a garden armchair, he talked politics with some members of the Institute of Gubbio. The situation was grave. War was feared. The State of Gubbio was involved in a system of collective security, which had appeared up until then an unbreakable diplomatic document. But for some time the powerful neighboring republic of Caporetto had been arming formidably, and it was feared she might be tempted to denounce her nonaggression pact with Gubbio. In fact, she sought to pick quarrels with all her neighbors. The Podesta

proclaimed once more Gubbio's desire for peace, but also his unbreakable decision to fight to a finish if he failed with his diplomacy of concession.

"We will not yield to threats. We do not wish our children to live under the sign of fear," said he in his grave voice, with the lilting accent of Gubbio.

Meanwhile the children played at Truth and Consequences. The master of the play called:

"Do armchairs fly?"

Formicella raised her hand in the affirmative. She had lost.

Not at all. An armchair might very well fly.

All the children cried: "Formicella, you are tricking us."

But she was obstinate. She sat at the Wolf's feet, and leaning toward him whispered in his ear. The Holy Wolf obediently lifted his right paw, and they saw without any possible doubt whatever, the Podesta's armchair, with the Podesta in it, leave the earth all by itself and positively take flight. Poor Podesta. He was in a tight corner, his living space was suddenly reduced to this cushion of Venetian tapestry on which he was seated. The armchair kept on flying. In some minutes the Podesta inspected the whole city of Gubbio with a steeply downward view. Then the armchair descended and came gently to rest in the place it had been. Formicella pretended that she saw nothing unusual about it. But the Wolf had departed. He wasn't very proud; it was his fifth miracle.

"Careful, now, only two more. I must pay attention to what I do," he said.

FORMICELLA began to grow up. She was nearly a young lady. She became more and more beautiful. She had not yet become fully accustomed to her beauty, for such a short time ago she had been so ugly. But she had now the most beautiful room of the house, and the evidence of a mirror each morning, which had a fixed place in her boudoir. She knew how to use her charm, and through it to dominate. Like power, like fortune, like crime, like even heroism, beauty has its fatality, which encloses beings thus endowed in a dangerous loneliness. For, after all, what can a very beautiful young girl really know of the world? She always sees people in their desire, or their vanity, but never in their real natures. Such, henceforth, was the destiny of Formicella, and she put the yoke on all those around her. She had become a despot. The Holy Wolf submitted also to this fascinating domination. He did all that she asked.

The family of Formicella wished to celebrate the anniversary of the day, as she had put it, that she had been healed of her ugliness. It was a splendid fete in the gardens and it was prolonged until late into the night. The Podesta came, and all the young people of the town. They had engaged musicians and there was much

dancing to the sound of the mandolins. The Holy Wolf was, of course, in the party. Formicella wanted him to dance. And he danced. Poor Wolf. He was much applauded. He had drunk a little too much champagne and he didn't know very well what he was doing. Towards midnight Formicella wanted some fireworks but none had been provided. She took the Holy Wolf aside and explained the situation. The Holy Wolf resisted; he regretted the incident of the armchair. He sensed confusedly that this power had not been given to him to be used for all these silly caprices. But she was so gentle, so suppliant, and the elasticity of his resolution was a little extended by the champagne, so he surrendered and solemnly raised his paw. Never before was seen anything so beautiful.

At first the set pieces of flowers. The chrysanthemums shone like suns and the avenue of rose bushes seemed a parade of constellations. Then the trees illuminated. Each branch, each leaf was incandescent. All flamed and nothing burned. Immense showers of fire bloomed in the sky and dispersed far away. The mandolins and the violins poured out enthralling music. Formicella danced. Danced until she was breathless. The miracle lasted more than an hour. It was the sixth, and the next to the last. Now only one. The Podesta was disgusted with the Wolf for wasting his miracles at a time when the country was in danger. He took the Wolf aside and advanced all the reasons of state which militated henceforth in favor of a certain discretion. The Wolf motioned that he understood. He passed a restless night. The remonstrance of the Podesta had spoiled the fete for him.

It was true just the same that he had now but one miracle left. That one Formicella desired at any cost. Precisely because, being the last, it had the value of an immense possibility for an extraordinary revolution of the natural course of things. What would she invent, what futility would she try, with this all-power, what throw of the dice which might check Nature itself? Of course to no purpose. Solely that she might show that the order of nature could be altered just as the course of history and the face of the world was changed by Cleopatra's nose. Formicella rubbed her nose and cudgeled her brains. She used all her wiles, returning constantly to her pleading. She worked on him by ruse, by surprise, by menace, in play, by caresses, by fits of tears, by anger, and by the power of her smile. The Wolf of Gubbio had but one more miracle. He kept it for an important occasion. He remained inflexible. The confidences of the Podesta had impressed him. He felt very reproachful, and

[*40*]

told himself that St. Francis had not accorded him the gift of miracles for the amusement of a foolish little girl and besides, the country was in danger. That night he dreamed of carnage. Formicella simply mocked at the idea of the country's danger. To begin with, politics was not the concern of women. And then the gleaming certitude of her beauty made her regard such an eventuality with a light heart. Yes, truly Beauty is as dangerous as Money and Power: it uproots one's being from its good natural soil and abandons one in a deadly liberty.

Without declaration of war, one Sunday morning, the armies of Caporetto invaded Gubbian territory. The tocsin rang. The men embraced their wives and children, and went singing and covered with flowers to defend the sacred soil of their fatherland. But in a few days the fortifications were pierced. The enemy hordes rushed out onto the plains. One saw the sorrowful throng of refugees, then the vanquished army itself, which retreated to camp under the very walls of the capital. The Parliament of Gubbio sat day and night. One evening the Podesta, oratorically declaiming about the sacred soil of Gubbio, made a long speech, very patriotic and loyal, which finished with these words:

"Gentlemen, I know that Gubbio is eternal.

If it is said that our country may not be saved but by a miracle, I respond; very well, I await the miracle!"

All the assembly rose, sang the national anthem with indescribable emotion. And as a miracle was necessary, they went in search of the Holy Wolf. He came. The assembly gave him a long ovation. The Podesta named him publicly the Commander-in-Chief of the routed army. Then someone blew a bugle and they all sang the Song of Departure. The Wolf bounded to the ramparts and inspected all the camps. His appearance rallied the courage of the most craven. They ceased to talk treasonably but rather in terms of revenge. The old retired generals got out their wrinkled uniforms, donned them, and asked to serve under this impetuous chief. Each took a place at the head of some troops, and awaited the enemy with feet firm. The advance guard of the enemy appeared the same night. But they encountered such a stout resistance that they soon had enough and awaited the arrival of the main Caporettan army. The enemy general decided on a stage of siege. He commenced it, but the Holy Wolf had his own plan.

One night with a handful of brave ones, he left Gubbio by a tunnel unknown to the assailants, and came out in the open country behind the besiegers.

He left his little band in some thick woods and went alone into the enemy camp. He glided between the tents until he came to that of the enemy's general-in-chief. He jumped on the sentinel and strangled him properly, before he had the time to say "Oof!" He slid under the tent and throttled the general in his bed. There was a young greyhound, elegant and white, who began to bark. It was she who gave the alarm, too late. The officers buckled their belts or suspended their swords at their sides, and arrived in haste at the general's tent to get their orders. The Wolf awaited them eagerly, and soon one after the other they were stiff in death. And then he himself began to bay furiously. His brave band bounded into the camp shouting horrible cries. The garrison of Gubbio made a sortie and overwhelmed the camp. It was a terrible massacre. The great and beautiful army, that marvelous modern army of Caporetto, vanished in smoke and blood, and the sun arose on an immense field of corpses.

That day the Holy Wolf truly knew glory. The joy of the deliverance plunged Gubbio into an incredible collective hysteria.

Everybody was at the windows or in the street when, at the end of the day, with Generalissimo Wolf at their head, the victorious army re-entered the town. All the bells rang, all the streets were decked with bunting, there were arches of triumph and bands everywhere. The noise went up to the heavens, from thousands of faces, strained and swollen hysterically, shouting, laughing, crying. The spontaneous joy of a whole community can be as impressive a spectacle as a forest fire or a cloudburst. It was obviously the Holy Wolf who received a good part of all these acclamations. This victory was his work. He came out, it must be added, exhausted, bleeding, a frightful red foam at the corner of his mouth, and the right paw, the miraculous paw, broken by the blow of a lance. Was this a sign that the grace of St. Francis had been withdrawn from him? Was it not, after all, his seventh and last miracle?

The Podesta couldn't resist the opportunity to deliver another speech. He felicitated the Wolf, clothing him solemnly with the gold-starred tunic of the Marshals of Gubbio, decreed that the great Plaque of National Gratitude be bestowed upon him, and thanked him in eloquent terms for having consecrated his seventh and last miracle to the salvation of the fatherland. It is unbelievable how often politicians lack perspicacity. The Wolf alone knew the nature of this victory. If he had been able to respond and explain, he would have revealed that there was not the least miracle involved in this overwhelming victory, but solely his wolfly courage, his warrior propensities, which he accomplished simply by becoming his former self. But he could not speak. On reflection, it was better so, as the continuation of our story will prove.

Anyway, he had above all the desire to bed down, to rest. When he turned to go he saw on his heels the greyhound of the Caporettan general, who had followed him proudly, as though it were she who had been decorated. The Wolf had never liked household dogs. But this day he was both magnanimous and fatigued. He took pity on her and led her with him into Formicella's house.

Although it was already dark there was no one in the house. Everyone was dancing in the streets under the light of Chinese lanterns. The Wolf was truly at the end of his strength. "That they have made me a Marshal is all very well. They would have done better to wash me and dress my wounds."

He knew that he was able to heal himself with his seventh and last miracle. But he preferred to hold it in reserve. He finished by going to sleep, the greyhound nearby.

AT THE END of the night, thirst and atrocious suffering awoke him. He had lost a great deal of blood. He was blow-beaten everywhere on his body. He had not strength enough to rise and drink. He was exhausted. The whole house slept very late. It was clear that no one thought of him. The greyhound arose, rummaged about the rooms, and disappeared. Anyway, he didn't care a fig about the greyhound. He thought that he should go and say good morning to Formicella. Any other morning he would have pushed open the door of her room, stretched out on the foot of the bed awaiting her awakening. But this morning—it was physically impossible. She would have to come to see him. It was the greyhound who by chance entered her room. With the insolence of very domesticated animals she bounded onto the bed and awoke Formicella, who found her very gentle, a beautiful dog, clean and perfumed, and delightful to play with. When the young girl was clothed, coifed, and made up, she thought of the Wolf and asked about him. They told her that he was badly wounded and that he appeared to be suffering greatly. She went to see him but recoiled at seeing him so dirty, bleeding, so lamentable. He regarded her with his kindly eyes. She had not the will to embrace him, but ordered that he be washed and cared for.

The Holy Wolf was a long time recovering. He was very feeble, and remained long days bedded in a corner of the house. Formicella seemed kind. She came to see him each morning and night. But she was really indifferent. She was invited to all the ceremonies, all the balls with which this miracle-given victory was celebrated. It is always thus. They are never the same—those who gain the battles and those who celebrate the victories. He remained alone then, all through the day. On her side, Formicella had acquired the habit of expecting companionship. The Wolf being unavailable, she took the greyhound. All the more willingly because this white greyhound was truly very nice, very distinguished. The greyhound's experience in the General Staff had taught her a strict discipline. She was an entertainer, a very knowing dog. One would never believe that a dog could have so many tricks in its bag. It was true that she didn't play chess, but she skipped rope, juggled with lighted candles, balanced herself on turning barrels, and had a thousand drolleries. Obviously she didn't perform miracles. But the Holy Wolf, or so they believed, could no longer perform them either. After all, this Wolf was less interesting than had been thought. And why had he been wounded? Didn't he have the miraculous power to protect himself? When one works a miracle one shouldn't do it by halves. There was something obscure there. Could it be that God would permit his paw—his supernatural paw—to be broken in battle if the Wolf had remained loyal to his oath? Yes, there was the question: Did they know that he had not broken his oath? For he had killed, had torn the throats of scores of men. All those who had seen him in battle spoke of him in admiration mixed with horror. It was understood, of course, that he had the right, as this war was just; that he was the Generalissimo and that his victims were the enemy. But finally it had to be admitted that he had not lost the taste of warm blood. Henceforth it would be necessary perhaps to be more careful of him. Were they actually secure with a beast so ferocious inside the walls of the town?

Formicella was, above all, vexed that the Holy Wolf, as she believed, had wasted his seventh and last miracle. And for what? For war. An affair which after all didn't concern her. And now this simpleton had no more miracles at his disposition. He was not at all amusing. She said to him one night, in a carelessly amiable tone:

"My poor Wolf. Look at you now. You are just a beast like the others."

He felt it bitterly. To begin with, he still had his seventh miracle. And then, even without miracles, it seemed to him that a wolf was not just a beast like the others, especially a wolf friend of St. Francis. He was in any case more valiant than all the men of Gubbio, who had fled before the Caporettans. She had said "a beast like the others." Ah, what a weight he had on his heart. He had shown her that he was not a beast like the others—and he could show her again. What did he have in common, for example, with that pale greyhound, that cunning dog, that flattering clown, that perfumed courtesan, that dog servant with soft ears? In the morning he strangled the greyhound.

POOR unfortunate Wolf. He had no sooner committed this murder than he repented it. It was unpremeditated. He thought of St. Francis and their mutual oath with his paw placed in the hand of the Saint. This time the grace of God had surely abandoned him. He lay in a corner, his nose between his paws. Two bitter tears rolled from his eyes and he began to groan. He could have eaten the greyhound, and so removed all trace of his sin, but he was too honest for that. Besides, what good would it do when his heart was broken?

Formicella heard his groan and came to see what troubled him. When she saw her dog bleeding and motionless, she became pale with fury. Her eyes, so large, so beautiful, flamed, glaring at the Wolf: "Oh—you monster!" said she.

And she fled like one crazed.

"He has killed my greyhound—my love of a dog. He has broken his promise. He is an assassin, a perjurer. He will kill us all if we don't take precautions."

The people were indignant. "A Holy Wolf?" Ah, no—a savage beast remains always just a savage beast.

"He might strangle us all, received as he is in our houses. Oh, the double-dealing rascal. What justification had he? The scoundrel. If we do not kill him he will kill us."

Actually it would be rather easy to kill him as long as he was bedridden and had not completely recovered from his wounds. The Podesta hastily called the whole garrison and even the firemen. The boys took sticks and forks and the crowd arrived before the house shouting cries of death. The Wolf heard and went to the window. The cries redoubled, a volley of pebbles broke the windowpanes. The Holy Wolf watched the crowd and believed that his heart would burst from sorrow and disillusionment. Ah, if he had not been, despite the murder of the greyhound, still bound by his promise to St. Francis, how he would delight in showing these puppets just what a Wolf is—a real Wolf. How he would have loved to scatter them in the streets, bolting like rabbits. And of a sudden the smell of his natal forest was borne to him by the wind. He sensed that he was not, that he had never been, of this world here, this cowardly mean world, egoistic and lying, lying, lying. He remembered his seventh miracle. But this murder! Had it not removed his power? If so he was lost, for never would he defend himself—remain bound to

crime. He invoked St. Francis in his heart, asking for mercy and protection. It would be shameful to be beaten to death with sticks.

Suddenly the crowd became silent with amazement. All the inhabitants of Gubbio saw, saw with their own eyes, the Wolf, their Wolf, rise slowly in the sky and move toward the forest. There was consternation. What! He still had another miracle! Did he have the perpetual power to perform them? What a loss they had sustained in letting him go!

"For it is we who have driven him away. It was you, Formicella, who excited us against him. You who owed him everything, whom he healed of your ugliness. Leave us, for you have a heart as perfidious as your face is beautiful!"

Formicella was terribly frightened. She flew to her room and cried, her face against the pillow. She cried all the day and all the night. It was a lot for a girl so beautiful.

THE WOLF had landed in the very middle of the forest on a tall oak. He had no wish to descend, ever. He remained perched there. Why should he ever come down? To find his food? But he had promised not to kill. There remained to him the mushrooms and the wild strawberries, but they were not at all to his taste. He decided to perish of hunger. There he was, seated on a high fork of a tree and steeped in sadness.

To say that he regretted the death of the greyhound was not exactly correct. He regretted the breaking of his oath; to have lost, before St. Francis, his wolfly honor. The inhabitants of Gubbio, the Podesta at their head—he despised them with all the weight of his heavy rancor. He knew them too well. Why had he not allowed them to be swallowed up by the earthquake, or let them perish by the sword! Did he still love Formicella? Oh, that face, beautiful as the sun! He had devoted himself to all her caprices. He had debased his gift of miracle-making for her. The degradation of a person is never sudden. It is prepared over a long time by multiple laxities and indulgences. He as wolf, the Citizen Wolf of Gubbio, the faithful friend of St. Francis, never should he have yielded to the fantasies of a little, vain young girl. It was there that it had all commenced. When he thought of all the champagne that they had made him drink, of the bottles he had uncorked, of the dances he had performed, of the armchair of the Podesta, of the fireworks, shame filled his heart. He sensed his soul filled with sins, and as he could not undo them, he determined to die. He would never pardon all these people for degrading him, a wolf, to the rank of a buffoon.

The night fell and the moon rose, round and cold. The Wolf watched it through the branches. He came to hate it, and shouted at it furiously, clamoring for death. The song, harsh and lugubrious, filled the forest and all the countryside. All the nightingales were stilled. The birches trembled on the shore of the pond. The hares of the fields reentered their tunnels. In their beds little children had nightmares and awoke crying. The Wolf continued to howl, and ancestral anger and ferocity entered his lamentation. The people of Gubbio understood what a malediction was being cried against them from the heart of the woods.

The next day there was a grand beating of the woods by all the villagers, not now to kill the Wolf, but to ask his pardon and to persuade him to return. The Wolf didn't move. No one had the idea to look above. Formicella passed under the oak, calling him in her sweetest voice. The

Wolf felt urged to respond to her call. He wanted to descend, but he refrained. His heart was broken, never to be mended.

The night following he continued to bay at the moon. And thus night after night.

ONE NIGHT he was interrupted in his funereal baying by an immense joyous sound which made the whole heavens vibrate. It was the bells of Gubbio, which rang at full volume. He remembered that they never rang thus in the middle of the night except for the Yuletide. He recalled the sermons of St. Francis of Assisi, the lovely manger that he made in the church, the beautiful peace promised to men of good will; even to the animals of the field and the birds of the sky. To himself even, poor Wolf. Then the Wolf of Gubbio in deep humility prayed in his heart to St. Francis to bring him into the grace of Noel. He experienced suddenly a profound nostalgia of love, of the desire to reconcile himself to, and to confide himself in, God. He descended from his tree and wended his way down the somber paths toward Gubbio. The bells had finished ringing. He proceeded down deserted streets. His former companions the shepherd dogs sensed him pass; they recognized him and barked with joy in the barnyards. That gave him pleasure; brave dogs! He arrived at the church, which was full of light and song. He dared not enter but waited in the shadow of the porch for the moment of the Elevation. He knew that then each would incline the head and no one would notice

him enter. The hand-bell of the altar boy sounded. The door was half open. He glided into the church, creeping low along the side aisle, and came to rest softly under the manger, his nose outside to see and to breathe the incense, the warm odor of the House of God. His soul filled with well-being.

At the moment of the Communion, he saw all the faithful rise to go to the holy table. They passed before him. He recognized all and each. And again he sensed a bitter flood fill his heart. He had suffered too much. Men are so ungrateful. How can God endure them? He saw Formicella. How beautiful she was, with her eyes lowered, her hands joined, her madonna-like hands. The faithful, after communicating, returned to pass again before him. And then there was an extraordinary thing, more marvelous than all the miracles. Each time that a faithful, carrying the Body of God that he had just received, passed before the manger, the Wolf could not but adore the majesty of this Presence and all his pain melted deliciously in his heart and in his being. It appeared to him that his wolfly soul participated in this communion, in this peace extending over all. He benefited, he also, from this divine Presence.

The music rose. A violin expressed the purity and the serenity of this grace. At a given moment, the Wolf sensed, when the musician returned the bow, that the lingering note had ended and his heart, his old savage heart, resisted no more and broke from an overflowing of sweet serenity. The violinist commenced a new bow-stroke. The Wolf groaned very softly. He was dead.

The Mass was finished and the children encircled the manger to venerate it. One of them noticed the nose of the Wolf under the manger. They respectfully removed his poor dead body. His mouth was full of honey. They cried, again a miracle! But if it was a miracle it was but the effect of Charity, sovereign, all powerful, and very precious Charity.

THIS EDITION *has been set in Fournier type,* *printed on Strathmore Text by the Quinn & Boden* *Company, Inc., and designed by Alvin Eisenman*